George Washington's Army

and Me

Story & Pictures
by Michael Dooling

To Kevin, Juliette and Allison

The author would like to thank Lauren Radecsky, Douglas Bender, Tim and Anissa Mitchell, their two children, Tim and Hannah and all the members of the 6th Pennsylvania Regiment a living history organization of the American Revolution.

It was a loud exciting sound. The fife and drum corps played Yankee Doodle Dandy as George Washington's Army marched in step. Cannons, cattle, sheep, and baggage wagons pushed along following the army. Women and children straggled behind. I followed because my Pa was one of the soldiers. My Ma died when I was a baby, and I had nowhere else to go. Some of the women looked after me, but mostly, I was on my own.

We camped in an open field surrounded by woods
and farmland, and it reminded me of home. Soldiers set
up a city of tents, but we set our belongings on the ground.

Besides Pa's 6th Pennsylvania Regiment, there were folks from nearly all thirteen colonies. Like me, almost everyone was far from home.

Pa and I used to live on a farm near Philadelphia. Nine months ago, the British army came and robbed us of everything we owned. They stole our cow, chickens, and corn crop. They even smashed our furniture. Pa was so angry we left that day, and he joined the 6th Pennsylvania Regiment. "Some day we'll go back, Elijah," Pa said. Hoping for that day was all I thought about.

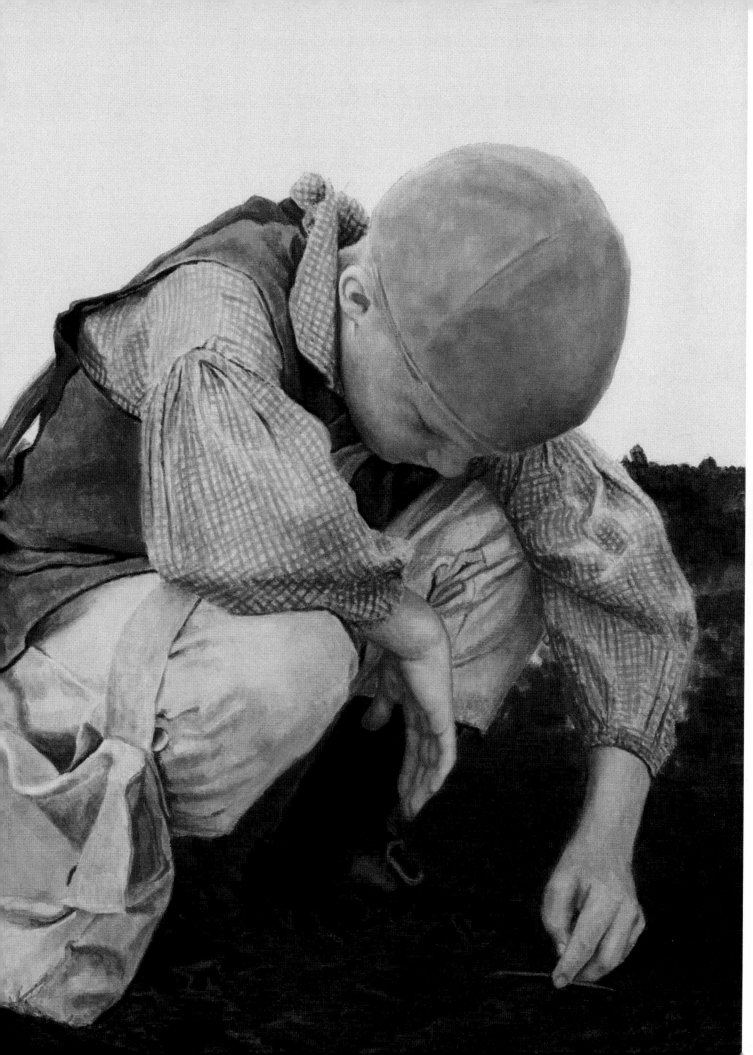

Often there was scarcely enough to eat. Sometimes we were blessed with hard biscuits, salted beef, and spruce beer made from the twigs of a spruce tree. I could hardly stomach the beer, but Pa said it was good for me. It warded off scurvy. Back home we would have feasted on cornmeal mush, fritters, meat pudding, ginger biscuits, and johnnycakes. But all those mighty fine meals seem so long ago.

After supper Pa and I played our favorite game, Draughts. I won although I suspect he let me. "King me!" I cried as I jumped his piece. Pa laughed. "Don't King me! We're fighting not to be 'Kinged' by King George of England."

Pa told me why we were fighting for independence from the British government. For years colonial Americans had been British subjects, and they had been forced to pay unfair and high taxes. When the colonists in Boston protested, British troops were sent to control the rioting. A shot was fired, and war broke out. "Get some sleep," Pa said. "We'll play again tomorrow."

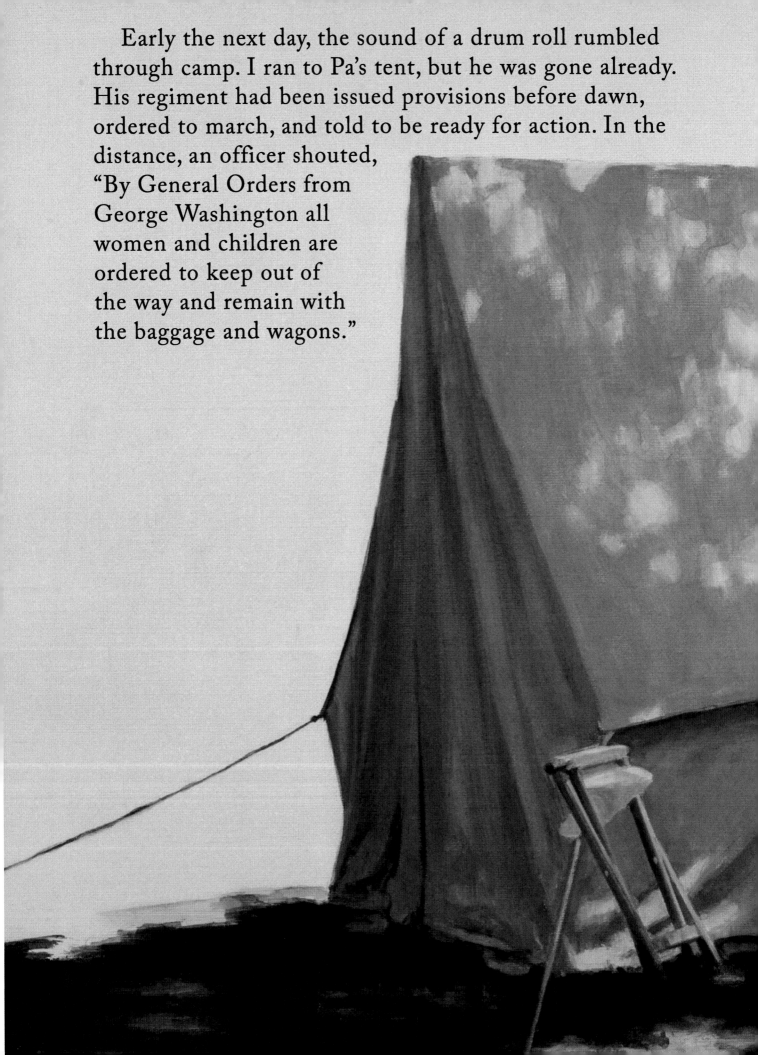

Early the next day, the sound of a drum roll rumbled through camp. I ran to Pa's tent, but he was gone already. His regiment had been issued provisions before dawn, ordered to march, and told to be ready for action. In the distance, an officer shouted, "By General Orders from George Washington all women and children are ordered to keep out of the way and remain with the baggage and wagons."

Suddenly, from the other side of the trees, a roar of cannon fire exploded!

A tremendous exchange of cannonade began. Smoke pillared above the treetops. The leaves shook! Amidst the chaos, women hurriedly carried buckets of water from our camp to the battlefield to cool off the cannons. With each trip, they returned with news about the fighting. Our troops had marched down a valley and passed through thick woods into an open field. Ahead, waiting for them, was a red-coated mass of British soldiers.

The deafening noise of the cannon fire seemed endless, and the volley of musketry went on and on. Cannon shot landed all around our men. The battle raged for hours. At dusk, the British retreated and fled north. That night, I barely slept worrying about Pa.

The next morning, cheers erupted proclaiming, "The British are gone! The British are gone!" I heard cries and moans from the wounded. Many of the men were overcome by heat exhaustion, and a soldier from the 6th Pennsylvania was carried into camp with a musket ball lodged in his thigh. I had to look away.

I overheard someone say, "Many soldiers are missing."

Pa was one of the missing. For hours we waited. As soldiers straggled into camp, I asked each one, "Have you seen my Pa? Have you seen my Pa?" They just shook their heads. I ran from tent to tent, and asked if anyone had seen him. Nobody had.

I had to find him. For hours, I searched the woods and fields. Little evidence of the battle remained except for trampled grass, pieces of cannonball, and the faint smell of gunpowder. The wounded and dead had been carried off hours earlier. I knew the women would be worried about me, but I couldn't go back to camp without Pa.

"Pa!" I called out. "Pa! Pa!"

It was getting late when I found an old abandoned barn.
Tired, hungry, and holding back tears, I thought about
giving up when the barn door creaked open, and someone
stumbled out and grabbed me. "Elijah, is that you?"
he whispered hoarsely.

"Pa!" I cried out. He had injured his leg during the battle and barely had the strength to stand up. I handed him my canteen and a hard biscuit I had saved. Separated from his regiment he had made his way here, but without food or drink, he was too weak to go any further. I was so relieved to see my Pa alive. That night, we slept in the barn and hugged each other until daybreak.

In the morning, we hobbled back to camp. Pa used his musket as a crutch, and I put my arm around his waist helping him walk. Getting home didn't seem so important anymore.

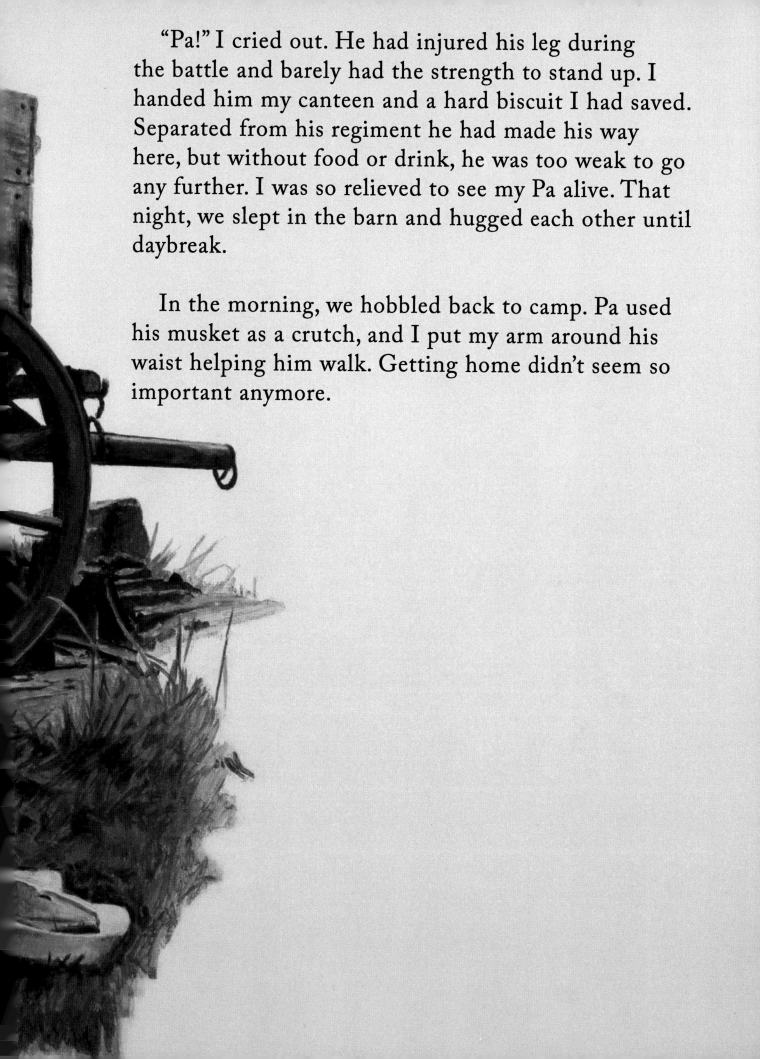

A few days later, we were ordered to break camp and move out. Once more George Washington's Army marched to the sound of the fife and drum. Pa marched, and I followed. At night we played Draughts, and Pa always won. I suspect that he knew I let him.